By **Brittany Quintero,**

Dartavius Washington,

and **Don'nayah Harris**

Tiffany and the Two Missing Teeth

Illustrated by **India Valle**

Reach Incorporated | Washington, DC

Shout Mouse Press

Reach Education, Inc. / Shout Mouse Press
Published by
Shout Mouse Press, Inc.

Shout Mouse Press is a nonprofit writing and publishing program dedicated to amplifying unheard voices. This book was produced through Shout Mouse writing workshops and in collaboration with Shout Mouse artists and editors.

Shout Mouse Press empowers writers from marginalized communities to tell their own stories in their own voices and, as published authors, to act as agents of change. In partnership with other nonprofit organizations serving communities in need, we are building a catalog of inclusive, mission-driven books that engage reluctant readers as well as open hearts and minds.

Learn more and see our full catalog at www.shoutmousepress.org.

Copyright © 2018 Reach Education, Inc.
ISBN-13: 978-1945434976 (Shout Mouse Press, Inc.)
ISBN-10: 194543497X

This book is dedicated
to everyone who doesn't like
how they look in the mirror.
Love yourself,
and smile every day.

All her life, people told Tiffany that her smile brightened their day.

She loved hearing that.

She loved the attention.

She loved bringing people happiness.

And Tiffany loved ballet dancing, too.
At every recital, she was the one with the biggest smile.

On the day of Tiffany's winter ballet performance, she was so nervous and so excited. She couldn't even think.

At lunch, Tiffany ate an apple, her favorite fruit. She was very hungry, and she took the biggest bite. Juice dripped down her chin.

But then she realized something was wrong...

She felt a cool breeze on the roof of her mouth.
Her two front teeth were missing!
"Oh No No No," she said.

Tiffany ran to the bathroom and looked in the mirror. Her smile looked like a jack-o-lantern gone wrong.

"Oh No No No," she said again.

Tiffany's friends had lost their teeth, but never two at once. And never on the day of the recital!

She tried to put her teeth back in, but they fell right back out again. Her smile was ruined.

Tiffany imagined what people would say when she went on stage. She started to cry.

Tiffany put her teeth in her pocket and wiped her eyes.

If I keep my mouth closed, no one will ever see my terrible smile, Tiffany thought.

I won't smile.

I won't laugh.

I won't talk.

I won't do anything.

But during art that afternoon, Tiffany's best friend Billy noticed something was wrong.

"You always smile in art class," Billy said.

Tiffany shook her head and put it down on the desk.

Billy said "knock knock," but Tiffany didn't respond.
"Don't make me do it," Billy said. "You know I'll do it!"
Billy made his best wacky face.
Tiffany busted out laughing.

Billy's eyes widened. "Whoa!" he said.

Tiffany stopped laughing. She closed her mouth. Then she took her teeth out of her pocket and showed them to Billy.

"Ew," Billy said, "your teeth are in your hand. They look so weird. They look like mini-marshmallows."

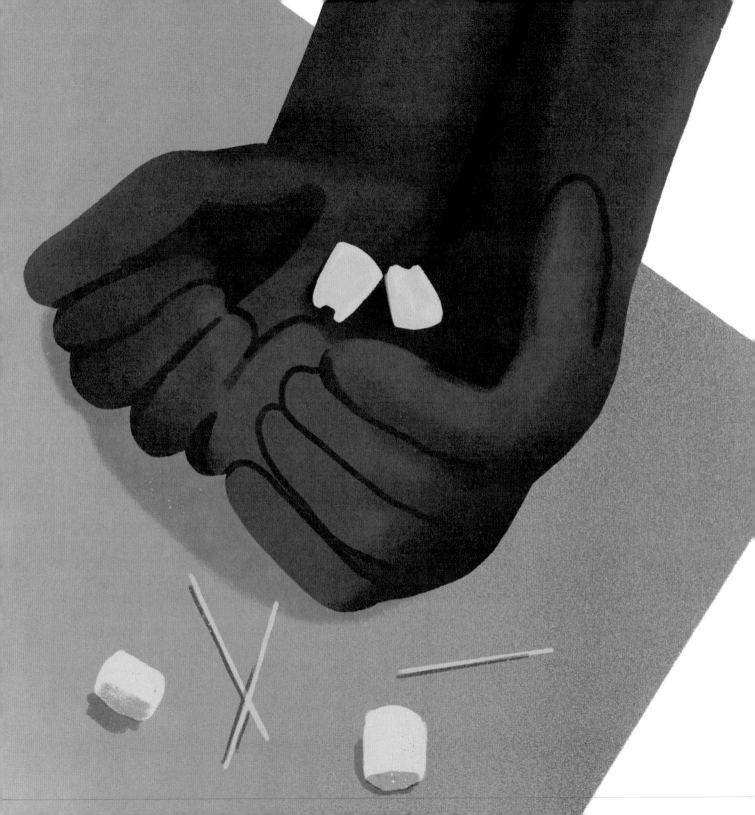

"Not funny," Tiffany said.

For the art project, they were building snowmen out of marshmallows. Tiffany looked at her teeth, and looked at the marshmallows. She picked up two and shoved them in the empty spaces in her mouth.

Maybe this will work, she thought.

Just then, Nico came over. He was the biggest,
toughest, rowdiest boy in her class.

"Give me some marshmallows," he said.

Tiffany started to say, "I won't have enough," but two
sticky, chewy marshmallows dropped onto her tongue.
Tiffany swallowed them.

"Are you eating something?" Nico asked.

Tiffany shook her head.

"Open your mouth," Nico said.

Tiffany ignored him. Nico pinched her.

"Ouch!" Tiffany said, but Nico saw her tongue between her teeth.

He fell on the floor laughing.

His laughter shook the whole school.

Tiffany slumped in her chair, looking like a dog who had been left at the park. She tried not to think about Nico.

"Don't be sad," Billy said. "Today is your recital. You have been practicing so hard. You're going to be great."

Tiffany tried to smile, but it was not good enough. She looked back down.

Billy hugged her. "If you're sad, then everybody's sad."

But Tiffany was sad.

Billy couldn't do anything to change that. That night, she was supposed to stand center stage. She was the star! She had to smile. Her picture would be everywhere. Everyone would be able to see her.

Tiffany knew what she had to do.

She was not going to dance.

At the dance studio, Tiffany sat in the corner, alone.
The rest of the class was getting dressed. The recital
started in fifteen minutes.

Suddenly, the door swung open. There was Chloe. Chloe was Tiffany's best friend from ballet. She was nine and a half, and Tiffany wished she was her big sister.

"Where have you been?" Chloe asked. "I've looked everywhere."

Tiffany didn't respond. She didn't want Chloe to laugh at her.

"Your smile is my good luck charm," Chloe said.

Tiffany shook her head and turned away.

"My thmile doethn't work anymore," Tiffany lisped.

"Cool!" Chloe said. "You lost your teeth!"

"You think it'th cool????"

"Yes, of course!"

"Oh No No No, it'th therrible," Tiffany said. "You know these picthures are going to go on the danthe thchool flyers, and everyone ith going to thee me and laugh at me."

"Don't be silly. Your smile would be pretty without ANY teeth!" Chloe said. "You'll get new teeth soon anyway. Isn't it cool to feel older?"

Tiffany thought about the older girls in the class. She did look up to them...

"Besides, there's fun things about not having all your teeth. My mom is taking me out for milkshakes after the recital. I can show you all the fun ways you can play with the straw."

"That doeth thound fun," Tiffany said. "Come on, let'th go rock thith."

On stage, the curtains opened and the lights came up.

Tiffany stood in the front, and she remembered every step.

She had the best moves. She ran, she jumped, she did the most amazing twirl.

She stopped thinking about her teeth, and she smiled.

The cameras flashed, and Tiffany smiled bigger.

After the recital, Tiffany was glowing. She nailed it. Her cheeks hurt from grinning so much.

Everybody said nice things.

"I love the way you twirl, girl," said Billy.

"You were as a graceful as a swan," said her teacher.

"Your dancing was spectacular!" said Chloe's momma.

No one talked about her teeth...

...All they
saw was talent.

About the Authors

Brittany Quintero

is a tenth grader at Eastern Senior High School. She likes to take care of kids. She sings in her school choir and dances. This is her first children's book. She hopes readers learn from this book not to be shy, and that they can be themselves even on their worst days. They can always make the better of it. She wanted to write a children's book because she wanted to see how it felt to write for kids and to change how they view things.

Dartavius Washington

is a senior at Dunbar High School. He likes to play Fortnite and to draw. This is his third children's book with Reach and Shout Mouse. He also wrote *Drip, Drip: The Story of the Angry Sherbet* (2016) and *Madison, Sit Down!* (2017) He wrote this book because he was once a toothless child, and he hopes people can understand that everyone's smile is beautiful.

Eva Shapiro served as Story Coach for this book.

Hayes Davis served as Head Story Coach for this year's series.

About the Illustrator

India Valle

is an illustrator based out of Richmond, Va. She graduated from Virginia Commonwealth University with a BFA in Communication Arts in 2018, and has a passion for stories, character design, and children's illustration. In addition to being a freelance illustrator, India also works in early childhood education, and she loves when her work with children and her art can inform one another. She takes inclusiveness and creating positive imagery for underrepresented groups very seriously, and wants to continually explore how illustration can be a powerful tool to help young people of any background understand the complex experiences and emotions they have growing up. See more of India's work and contact her at indiavalle.com.

Writers and artists at work

Acknowledgments

For the sixth summer in a row, teens from Reach Incorporated were issued a challenge: compose original children's books that will both educate and entertain young readers. Specifically, these teens were asked to create inclusive stories that reflect the realities of their communities, so that every child has the opportunity to relate to characters on the page. And for the sixth summer in a row, these teens have demonstrated that they know their audience, they believe in their mission, and they take pride in the impact they can make on young lives.

Thirteen writers spent the month of July brainstorming ideas, generating potential plots, writing, revising, and providing critiques. Authoring quality books is challenging work, and these authors have our immense gratitude and respect: Talik, Synia, Jada, Temil, Trevon, Kahliya, De'Asia, India, Essence, Malik, Brittany, Dartavius, and Don'nayah.

These books represent a collaboration between Reach Incorporated and Shout Mouse Press, and we are grateful for the leadership provided by members of both teams. From Reach, John Gass contributed meaningfully to discussions and morale, and the Reach summer program leadership of Luisa Furstenberg-Beckman kept us organized and well-equipped. From the Shout Mouse Press team, we thank Head Story Coach Hayes Davis, who oversaw this year's workshops, and Story Coaches Holly Bass, Sarai Johnson, Barrett Smith, and Eva Shapiro for bringing both fun and insight to the project. We can't thank enough illustrators Jiaqi Zhou, Liu Light, West Cahall, and India Valle for bringing these stories to life with their beautiful artwork. Finally, Amber Colleran brought a keen eye and important mentorship to the project as the series Art Director and book designer. We are grateful for the time and talents of these writers and artists!

Finally, we thank those of you who have purchased books and cheered on our authors. It is your support that makes it possible for these teen authors to engage and inspire young readers. We hope you smile as much while you read as these teens did while they wrote.

Mark Hecker,
Reach Incorporated

Kathy Crutcher,
Shout Mouse Press

About Reach Incorporated  **Reach**

Reach Incorporated develops grade-level readers and capable leaders by preparing teens to serve as tutors and role models for younger students, resulting in improved literacy outcomes for both.

Founded in 2009, Reach recruits high school students to be elementary school reading tutors. Elementary school students average 1.5 grade levels of reading growth per year of participation. This growth – equal to that created by highly effective teachers – is created by high school students who average more than two grade levels of growth per year of program participation.

As skilled reading tutors, our teens noticed that the books they read with their students did not reflect their reality. As always, we felt the best way we could address this issue was to let our teen tutors author new books themselves. Through our collaboration with Shout Mouse Press, these teens create engaging stories with diverse characters that invite young readers to explore the world through words. By purchasing our books, you support student-led, community-driven efforts to improve educational outcomes in the District of Columbia.

Learn more at reachincorporated.org.